Jack in Search of Art

Jack
In Search
of Art

WRITTEN AND ILLUSTRATED BY

Arlene Boehm

ROBERTS RINEHART PUBLISHERS

BOULDER, COLORADO

This book is dedicated to the staff of the Delaware Art Museum.

All works are in the the collections of the Delaware Art Museum.

2 | **MISCHIEF NIGHT** by Jamie Wyeth F.V. DUPONT ACQUISITION FUND

7 | **DANCER** by Lin Emery GIFT OF TRAMMELL CROW COMPANY / © LIN EMERY/LICENSED BY VAGA, NEW YORK, NY

8, 9, 31, 32 | **ORIFICE II** by Joe Moss PURCHASED THROUGH GRANTS FROM THE LONGWOOD AND CRYSTAL FOUNDATIONS

10 | **THE MERMAID** by Howard Pyle GIFT OF THE CHILDREN OF HOWARD PYLE IN MEMORY OF THEIR MOTHER, ANNE POOLE PYLE

11 | **SMALL ACROBATS** by Tom Bostelle GIFT OF THE ARTIST

11 | **WORKING DRAWING #1: TENSION** by Gretchen Hupfel LOUISA DUPONT COPELAND MEMORIAL FUND

13 | **RIVER OF PONDS II** by Frank Stella PURCHASED THROUGH FUNDS PROVIDED BY THE NATIONAL ENDOWMENT FOR THE ARTS AND CONTRIBUTIONS / © FRANK STELLA / ARTISTS RIGHTS SOCIETY (ARS), NEW YORK

14, 26-27 | **BLACK CRESCENT** by Alexander Calder SPECIAL PURCHASE FUND / © ARTISTS RIGHTS SOCIETY (ARS), NEW YORK / ADAGP, PARIS

14 | **LONGHORN STEER, WESTERN SERIES, AMERICAN PREDELLA #6** by Don Nice PURCHASED THROUGH FUNDS PROVIDED BY THE NATIONAL ENDOWMENT FOR THE ARTS AND CONTRIBUTIONS

15 | **SPRINGHOUSE** by N.C. Wyeth SPECIAL PURCHASE FUND

16 | **A WOLF HAD NOT BEEN SEEN IN SALEM FOR THIRTY YEARS** by Howard Pyle HOWARD PYLE COLLECTION

16 | **AN ATTACK ON A GALLEON** by Howard Pyle MUSEUM PURCHASE

17 | **THE BUCCANEER WAS A PICTURESQUE FELLOW** by Howard Pyle MUSEUM PURCHASE

17 | **MONUMENT IN THE PLAZA** by John Sloan GIFT OF THE JOHN SLOAN MEMORIAL FOUNDATION

17 | **SUMMERTIME** by Edward Hopper GIFT OF DORA SEXTON BROWN

17 | **THE OLD VIOLIN** by Jefferson David Chalfant LOUISA DUPONT COPELAND MEMORIAL FUND

17 | **ANTHONY VAN CORLEAR, THE TRUMPETER OF NEW AMSTERDAM** Howard Pyle, designer; executed by Tiffany Studios F.V. DUPONT ACQUISITION FUND

18 | **DOCUMENTA** by Kenneth Noland PURCHASED THROUGH FUNDS PROVIDED BY THE NATIONAL ENDOWMENT FOR THE ARTS AND CONTRIBUTIONS © KENNETH NOLAND / LICENSED BY VAGA, NEW YORK, NY

18 | **PEACE THROUGH CHEMISTRY** by Roy Lichtenstein PURCHASED THROUGH FUNDS PROVIDED BY THE FRIENDS OF ART AND THE NATIONAL ENDOWMENT FOR THE ARTS © ESTATE OF ROY LICHTENSTEIN

18 | **BALLOONS** by Alexander Calder GIFT OF FORSTMANN-LEFF ASSOCIATES / © 1988 ARTISTS RIGHTS SOCIETY (ARS), NEW YORK / ADAGP, PARIS

18 | **WILD IRIS** by Isaac Witkin GIFT OF MRS. RICHARD CORROON

20, 21 | **ROME II** by Al Held F.V. DUPONT ACQUISITION FUND / © AL HELD/LICENSED BY VAGA, NEW YORK, NY

22, 25 | **VERONICA VERONESE** by Dante Gabriel Rossetti SAMUEL AND MARY R. BANCROFT MEMORIAL

22 | **LADY LILITH** by Dante Gabriel Rossetti SAMUEL AND MARY R. BANCROFT MEMORIAL

23 | **ISABELLA AND THE POT OF BASIL** by William Holman Hunt SPECIAL PURCHASE FUND

23 | **THE ARMING OF A KNIGHT** William Morris, designer; painted by Dante Gabriel Rossetti and William Morris ACQUIRED THROUGH THE BEQUEST OF DORIS WRIGHT ANDERSON AND THROUGH THE F.V. DUPONT ACQUISITION FUND

23 | **THE COUNCIL CHAMBER** by Edward Coley Burne-Jones SAMUEL AND MARY R. BANCROFT MEMORIAL

26 | **LION AT REST** by Abbott H. Thayer SAMUEL AND MARY R. BANCROFT MEMORIAL

26 | **BENCH AND TABLE** by Scott Burton F.V. DUPONT ACQUISITION FUND / © ESTATE OF SCOTT BURTON

27 | **RHUBARB** by Ben Schonzeit PURCHASED THROUGH FUNDS PROVIDED BY THE NATIONAL ENDOWMENT FOR THE ARTS AND CONTRIBUTIONS

28 | **RIOT** by Deborah Butterfield F.V. DUPONT ACQUISITION FUND

ROBERTS RINEHART PUBLISHERS
6309 Monarch Park Place
Niwot, Colorado 80503
Visit our web site at www.robertsrinehart.com

Distributed to the trade by Publishers Group West

Published in Ireland and the UK by
ROBERTS RINEHART PUBLISHERS
Trinity House, Charleston Road
Dublin 6, Ireland

Copyright © 1998 Arlene Boehm

Designed and illustrated by Arlene Boehm

ISBN 1-57098-244-9 casebound, ISBN 1-57098-234-1 softcover

Library of Congress Cataloging in Publication Data
Boehm, Arlene P.
    Jack in search of Art / written and illustrated by Arlene Boehm.
       p. cm.
      Summary: Jack the bear mistakes the sign announcing Art at the
museum for the name of another bear and while searching for him
discovers and appreciates beautiful things.
    ISBN 1-57098-244-9 (hardcover). – ISBN 1-57098-234-1 (softcover)
    [1. Bears—Fiction. 2. Art museums—Fiction. 3. Art
appreciation—Fiction. 4. Museums—Fiction.] I. Title.
PZ7.B635725Jag 1998
[E]—DC21   98-13995
                                      CIP
                                        AC

Splish!
Splash!
Splosh!
"Urg..." Jack groaned as he muddled through puddles of water and mud, "How can I get out of this rain?!"

Hmmm...Maybe I'll go there!
Jack thought.
Come See Art...but who is Art?
Art must be someone who
works here.

As he splashed toward the museum entrance, Jack thought...

...Art is lucky to work indoors.

Oh! How Art
must enjoy
working here!

"Where would I find Art?" Jack asked.

"Up the stairs, and to the left and to the right... or... up the elevator, and to the right and to the left," answered the Museum Bear with a smile.

I wonder how Art can be in *all* those places at the same time? thought Jack.

"Art?" Jack asked one bear...
"No...Nicholas is my name!"
said the bear with a smile.

"Art?" Jack asked another...
"No...I'm Vincent! Glad to
meet you!" this bear replied.

On and on, Jack met many
bears at the museum, but
still, not one bear was
named Art. He'd just
have to keep looking.

Hmmmm... Beautiful, beautiful
pictures, but no Art.

Art's not here either,
but many more pictures!
Some of them cub-size...

...and others, ROOM SIZE!
Pictures everywhere, but still no sign of Art.

When I find him, thought Jack, I will thank Art for all the beautiful things that I have discovered!

Then, Jack found the *most beautiful* pictures
he had ever seen!
If only Art were here, he thought, we could talk
on and on about the glorious pictures! And then,
before he knew it, the words just burst from him.
"Where is Art!?" he called out loudly in
the quiet gallery.

Oops! Too loud! Too loud! Jack did not mean to speak so loudly! The Museum Bear hurried over. "Oh, what have I done?!" whispered Jack to himself.

"May I help you?" the Museum Bear asked politely. Jack sighed with relief, "Oh yes, please. I am *still* looking for Art."

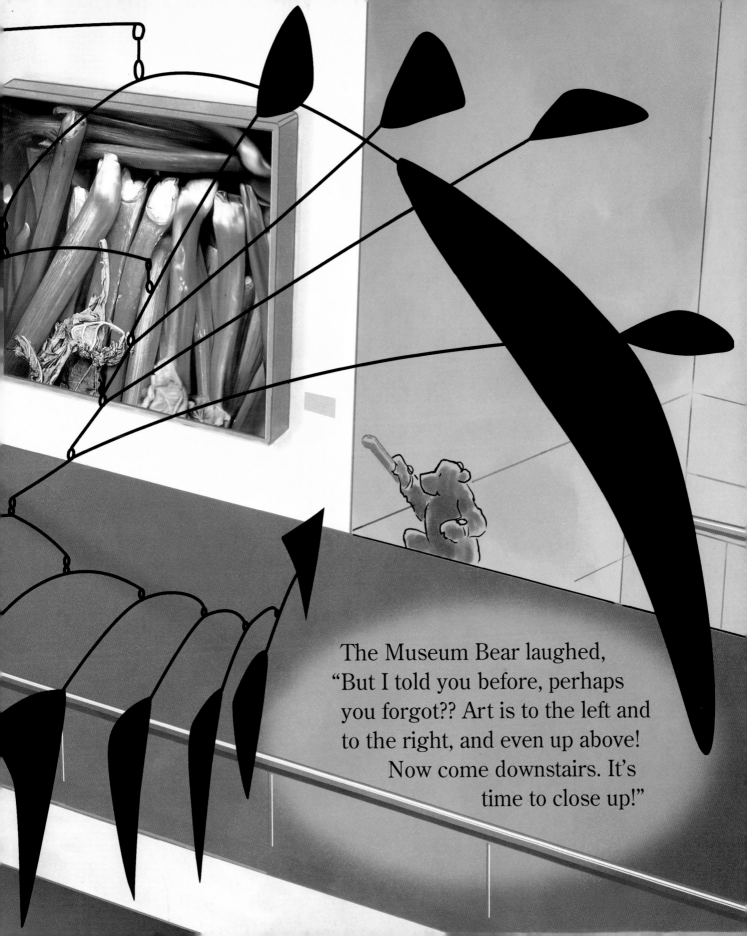

The Museum Bear laughed,
"But I told you before, perhaps
you forgot?? Art is to the left and
to the right, and even up above!
Now come downstairs. It's
time to close up!"

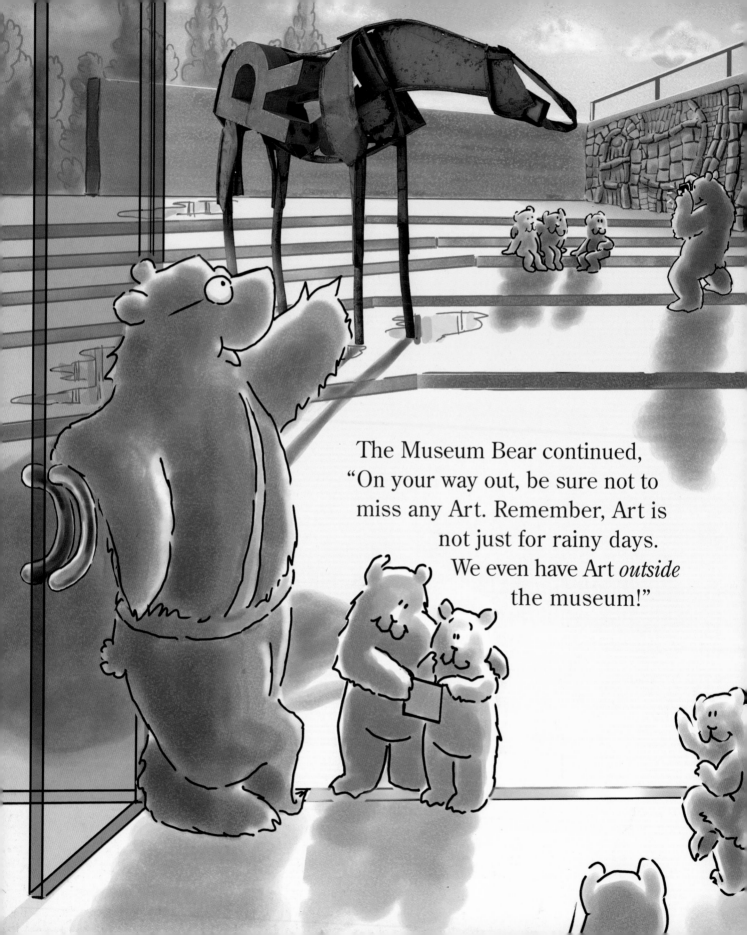

The Museum Bear continued,
"On your way out, be sure not to
miss any Art. Remember, Art is
not just for rainy days.
We even have Art *outside*
the museum!"

"You mean, all these beautiful
things are... *Art?!*" asked Jack.
"Yes!" the Museum Bear replied.
"Pictures to the left and to the right,
ALL ART!!!" cried Jack with delight.
"Yes! Yes!!!" said the Museum Bear.
"Oooooohhh!" said Jack, "I looked
and I looked but I didn't see! Art
was right in front of me!"
"Most certainly YES indeed!" the
Museum Bear smiled, and agreed.

Then Jack said, a little sadly,
"...So, Art is not a bear?..."

"Oh, I wouldn't say that..." answered the Museum Bear.
"Visit us again soon. And next time, if you'd like, we can
look at the Art together! Just ask for me at the desk."
"Oh, I'd like that very much!" said Jack.
"Who shall I ask for?"

With a wink
and a smile, the
Museum Bear
answered...

"Art!"